# Wildly Weird Weather

Gareth Stevens
PUBLISHING

# What's a Haboob?

By Therese M. Shea

Please visit our website, www.garethstevens.com. For a free color catalog of all our high-quality books, call toll free 1-800-542-2595 or fax 1-877-542-2596.

**Cataloging-in-Publication Data**

Names: Shea, Therese M.
Title: What's a haboob? / Therese M. Shea.
Description: New York : Gareth Stevens Publishing, 2024. | Series: Wildly weird weather | Includes glossary and index.
Identifiers: ISBN 9781538288061 (pbk.) | ISBN 9781538288078 (library bound) | ISBN 9781538288085 (ebook)
Subjects: LCSH: Sandstorms–Juvenile literature.
Classification: LCC QC958.S54 2024 | DDC 551.55'9–dc23

First Edition

Published in 2024 by
**Gareth Stevens Publishing**
2544 Clinton St.
Buffalo, NY 14224

Designer: Corinne Eberwine
Editor: Theresa Emminizer

Photo credits: Cover, John D Sirlin/Shutterstock.com; p. 5 Omer koclar/Shutterstock.com; p. 6 VectorMine/Shutterstock.com; p. 9 (inset) Rainer Lesniewski/Shutterstock.com; p. 9 Przemek Iciak/Shutterstock.com; p. 10 Lokibaho/iStockphoto.com; p. 13 andrekoehn/Shutterstock.com; p. 14 karenfoleyphotography/iStockphoto.com; p. 16 Sundry Photography/Shutterstock.com; p. 17 SpiffyJ/iStockphoto.com; p. 19 Edgar G Biehl/Shutterstock.com; p. 21 Lancho/Shutterstock.com.

Printed in the United States of America

CPSIA compliance information: Batch #CS24GS: For further information contact Gareth Stevens, New York, New York at 1-800-542-2595.

Find us on

# Contents

Words in the glossary appear in **bold** type the first time they are used in the text.

# Ha-what?

Picture yourself coming out of school. It's sunny. But across the soccer field, you see a wall of gray reaching from the sky to the ground. And it's moving toward you really fast. It looks like a huge wave of dust. What you see is a haboob—get inside!

If you've never heard of a haboob, you might not live in an area that often has them. More places have them than you might think, though! It's important to know the signs—and dangers—of this wild weather.

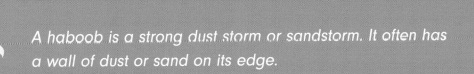

# That's a Fact!

The word "haboob" (hah-BOOB) comes from the **Arabic** word habb. It means to blow.

*A haboob is a strong dust storm or sandstorm. It often has a wall of dust or sand on its edge.*

All haboobs are dust storms or sandstorms, but not all dust storms and sandstorms are haboobs!

## How a Thunderstorm Forms

storm movement

Warm, wet air rises.

heavy rain

Cold air moves downward.

# Wow, a Wall!

Haboobs form from large thunderstorms in dusty or sandy places. Conditions must be just right, though.

For a haboob to form, the rain must evaporate, or dry up, as it falls in dry air. The air becomes even cooler and **denser.** This cold, dense air moves downward. It pushes out the air on the ground, which picks up dust and sand. When this happens with very large air masses, a moving wall of dust or sand can form.

 *Not every thunderstorm creates the large **outflow** of air that forms a haboob.*

# Around the World

Haboobs happen in flat, desert-like areas. They happen most often in the Sudan, an area to the south of a desert called the Sahara. In the summer, powerful winds blow across the Sahara. They're sometimes as fast as 70 miles (113 km) per hour! Haboobs in this area can be dangerous.

## That's a Fact!

Sudan is the name of a country as well as an area in Africa.

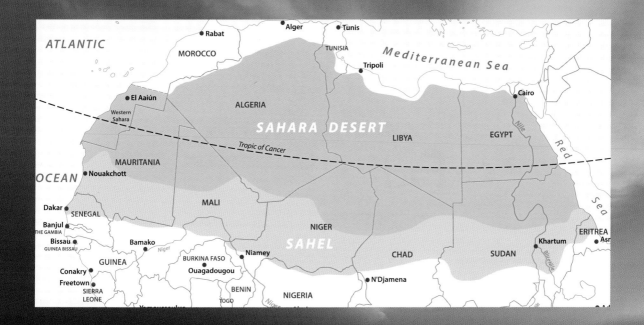

Most haboobs last a few hours. One in 2015 in the **Middle East** lasted days. It **affected** seven countries and killed 12 people. Haboobs also occur in Central Asia, China, Australia, and parts of North America.

 *The Sahara covers most of northern Africa and is the largest desert in the world. In fact, sahara means desert in Arabic.*

## That's a Fact!

Some haboobs are so large they can be seen from space!

# In the United States

Haboobs can happen in the United States. They're most likely to occur in the Southwest because the deserts there have a lot of sand and dust. When thunderstorm winds begin to blow in these areas, they can draw this matter up from the ground.

One of the largest haboobs on record in Arizona happened in 2011. It was thought to be about 5,000 feet (1,524 m) tall. Airplanes couldn't land at the Phoenix airport because it was so hard to see.

*This haboob formed near Phoenix, Arizona.*

# Caught in the Middle

What is it like to be in the middle of a haboob? Have you ever gotten sand in your eyes at the beach? It's like that—but much worse. Imagine high-speed winds spraying sand and dirt into your face. It would be hard to breathe!

Even people who remain inside during a haboob can feel its harmful effects. Winds push dust and sand through cracks in buildings. Those with **respiratory** problems should be careful in dust and sandstorms. The air can harm their health.

*Haboobs can also carry harmful **fungi** found in soil that can cause illnesses. Wearing a mask during a haboob can help.*

Haboobs are sometimes called "black blizzards" because, like snowstorms, they make **visibility** so poor.

# Safe in the Storm

If you're near a haboob, there are ways you can stay safe. First, try to stay away from the storm if you can.

Since visibility is poor during a haboob, car crashes can happen. If you're in a car, ask the driver to pull off the road as far as possible. Then, turn the car lights off. Why? Drivers often follow lights in front of them when weather is bad. They may follow you off the road—and hit your car—if the lights are on.

## That's a Fact!

A haboob's high winds can knock down power lines and trees. They also can cause harm to buildings.

# Predicting Them

Haboobs are hard to **predict**. But if a thunderstorm is predicted, a haboob is more likely. The National Weather Service (NWS) tries to let people know if one may happen.

The NWS issues, or announces, a dust storm watch if a dust storm is possible. It will issue a dust storm warning when the storm is happening. That means visibility will be less than 0.5 mile (0.8 km). Sand or dust in winds will blow more than 30 miles (48 km) an hour.

*Doppler radar*

Scientists use a tool called radar to track storms. Radar antennae send out waves of energy, or power, called radio waves. Waves return when they hit something.

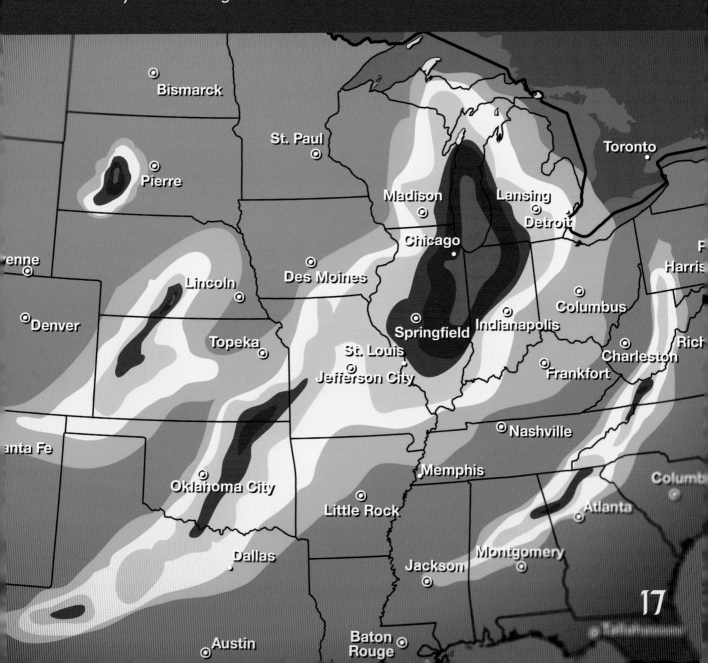

17

# More Haboobs?

Many scientists think it's likely more places will have haboobs in days to come. When people need land for farming or building, they clear land of trees and other plants. These plants have roots that keep soil in place. Without them, soil can blow around.

**Climate change** may also cause places to get hotter and have more **droughts**. Water sources may dry up. This too can cause plants to die and the land to become more like a desert. More deserts will create more chances for haboobs to form.

*A farmer looks at fields during a drought. Without rain, farmland can dry up and turn into loose soil.*

## That's a Fact!

Scientists studied the amount of dust in rainfall in the American West. They found out dust in rain has been increasing in many places, including Colorado and Utah.

# Traveling Dust

So far, no ways exist to prevent, or stop, storms like haboobs. But we do have ways to help nature and fight climate change.

Even if you don't live somewhere that has haboobs, you might still see their effects. When dust is taken up into Earth's **atmosphere**, it can travel hundreds of miles, ending up far away. For example, dust from the Sahara can end up in the Amazon rain forest. Haboobs remind us how powerful nature is!

*Dust on this car in Spain came from a storm in the Sahara!* ❯

## That's a Fact!

Kids can fight climate change too! Learn how at: climatekids.nasa.gov/how-to-help/.

# Glossary

**affect:** To create a change in something.

**Arabic:** A language originally spoken by people from the Arabian Peninsula and now spoken widely in the Middle East and northern Africa.

**atmosphere:** The mixture of gases that surround a planet.

**climate change:** Long-term change in Earth's climate, caused mainly by human activities such as burning oil and natural gas.

**dense:** Packed very closely together.

**drought:** A long period of very dry weather.

**fungus:** A living thing that is somewhat like a plant, but doesn't make its own food, have leaves, or have a green color. Fungi include molds and mushrooms.

**Middle East:** The area where southwestern Asia meets northeastern Africa.

**outflow:** The outward movement of something.

**predict:** To guess what will happen in the future based on facts or knowledge.

**respiratory:** Having to do with breathing or the parts of the body that are used in breathing.

# For More Information

## Books

Gendell, Megan. *Dust Storms.*Mendota Heights, MN: Apex Editions, 2023.

Perritano, John. *The Ultimate Book of Dangerous Weather.* Broomall, PA: Mason Crest, 2020.

Williamson, Margaret. *Dust Storms: Causes and Effects.* Mankato, MN: 12-Story Library, 2022.

## Websites

### Dust Storms
*ein.az.gov/hazards/dust-storms*
The Arizona Emergency Information Network provides links about what to do before, during, and after dust storms.

### Dust Storms and Haboobs
*www.weather.gov/safety/wind-dust-storm*
Find out what the National Weather Service wants you to know about these storms.

### Sandstorms
*www.weatherwizkids.com/?page_id=1333*
This Weather Wiz Kids site is a great review of storm facts.

# Index